DATE DUE

Karyn Henley

Illustrated by Susan Kathleen Hartung

Tyndale House Publishers, Inc.
Wheaton, Illinois

Visit Tyndale's exciting Web site at www.tyndale.com

Designed by Beth Sparkman

Edited by Betty Free

Library of Congress Cataloging-in-Publication Data

Henley, Karyn.
Rag baby / Karyn Henley.
p. cm.
Summary: After an adventure with her beloved doll, a young girl is reminded of God's love for everyone. Includes discussion questions and related Bible verses.
ISBN 0-8423-5434-4 (Hardcover : alk. paper)
[1. Dolls--Fiction. 2. Christian life--Fiction.] I. Title.
PZ7.H3895 Rag 2002
[E]--dc21 2001001286

Printed in China

07 06 05 04 03 02
7 6 5 4 3 2 1

Dear Reader,

Jesus often told stories called parables. Parables have special hidden meanings.

This story is a bit like a parable because it also has a special hidden meaning. The end of the story tells what the meaning is. That's so younger children will be able to understand it.

You older children may be able to figure out the meaning even before you read the end. Still, you may have questions.

Here are some Bible verses that will help you understand the answers to two questions you may have. You'll want to talk about these verses with a parent or an adult friend.

How do I know that God loves me?

Deuteronomy 31:8 — John 3:16-17

Psalm 145:8-20 — 1 John 4:9-10

What does it mean that God bought me and that I was made to belong to him?

Psalm 100:3 — 1 Corinthians 6:19-20

Isaiah 43:1 — Colossians 1:13-14

Enjoy the story!

Karyn Henley

Rag Baby sat on Jessie's bed beside Cat-Cat and Bella Elephant. He was soft and pudgy, made of a cotton pillowcase from Grandma's ragbag. Grandma had given him to Jessie on her second birthday. When everyone sang "Happy Birthday," Rag Baby felt like the song was for him, too.

At first Jessie took
Rag Baby everywhere.
He went to the grocery
store and the doctor's office,
to bookstores and restaurants.
He rode in car seats
and backpacks and beach bags.

But what Rag Baby liked best
was the way Jessie always
snuggled him close to her at night.

Grandma made other presents for Jessie too. There were sweaters and mittens and Jessie's favorite long, red-and-yellow-striped winter scarf.

As Jessie grew older, she outgrew her sweaters and mittens. But she still wore her red-and-yellow scarf in cold weather.

And Jessie still loved Rag Baby, even though she now let Rag Baby spend most of his days on top of her bed.

Cat-Cat and Bella Elephant were good company for Rag Baby. Whenever Jessie went away, they all jumped on the bed, looked at pictures in books, and played hide-the-sock. (But Bella Elephant always forgot where she hid the sock!)

One day Jessie plopped a suitcase onto her bed. *We're going on a trip!* thought Rag Baby. Jessie put shirts and shorts and socks into the suitcase. She put in her toothbrush and tooth-paste. But she did not pack Rag Baby.

Rag Baby slumped down into a sad heap. *Jessie's going on an adventure without me,* he thought. *Why can't I go too? Will Jessie ever take me on an adventure again?*

Jessie's mom closed the suitcase and locked it. "While you're at camp, I'll clean your closet and give away the clothes you've outgrown," said Mom. "I'll clean under your bed, too. Who knows what I'll find under there!"

"Lots of dust bunnies!" said Jessie, laughing. She tugged the suitcase off the bed and carried it out the door.

"What's a Dust Bunny?" asked Rag Baby.

"And why would it live *Under?*" asked Bella Elephant, shivering and covering her eyes.

"Have you ever been *Under?*" asked Cat-Cat.

"Yes!" said Bella Elephant.

"What was it like?" asked Rag Baby.

"I don't know," said Bella. "I was *Under* for only a minute when Jessie dropped me once. I closed my eyes and held my breath until she picked me up again."

"I've been *Under*," said Cat-Cat.

"You have?" said Rag Baby.

"Oh, yes," said Cat-Cat. "All night long!"

Bella gasped. "All night?"

"Yes!" said Cat-Cat. "I fell over the *Edge* one night. It was lonely and dark and cold."

"What did you see?" asked Rag Baby.

"A sock," said Cat-Cat. "It's a good place to go sock hunting."

Over the *Edge* and down *Under*. The more Rag Baby thought about it, the more he wanted to explore *Under*. Maybe he would meet the Dust Bunnies. Maybe they would like to come up *Above* to meet Cat-Cat and Bella Elephant.

"I'm going to do it. I'm going to explore down *Under*," Rag Baby said.

"Ooh!" said Bella. "Be very careful!"

"Great!" said Cat-Cat. "Maybe you'll find another sock!"

That night Rag Baby and Cat-Cat and Bella Elephant crept to the *Edge* and peeked over. It was a long drop down to the floor. But Rag Baby had been dropped many times. He knew it wouldn't hurt, because he was soft and pudgy and made of cotton. This would be a great adventure!

"Count to three with me," said Rag Baby.

So Cat-Cat and Bella Elephant counted with Rag Baby. "One, two, three . . ."

Tumble, tumble, over the *Edge*. Rag Baby plopped to the floor. He stood up and waved to Cat-Cat and Bella Elephant. Then the small and pudgy Rag Baby bravely marched *Under*.

Under was very dark. But not as dark as it was inside the toy box. At least there was a bit of light shining in from the hall. Rag Baby called, "Dust Bunnies, where are you?"

No one answered. Rag Baby slowly moved forward. He bumped into something big and hard. He pushed on it, and it rolled. "A ball!" said Rag Baby. He moved around the ball.

Pat, pat, pat. Under his feet was something smooth and flat. "A piece of paper," said Rag Baby.

Rag Baby walked a little farther until he touched what felt like rows of prickly grass. He giggled. "A hairbrush!" he said.

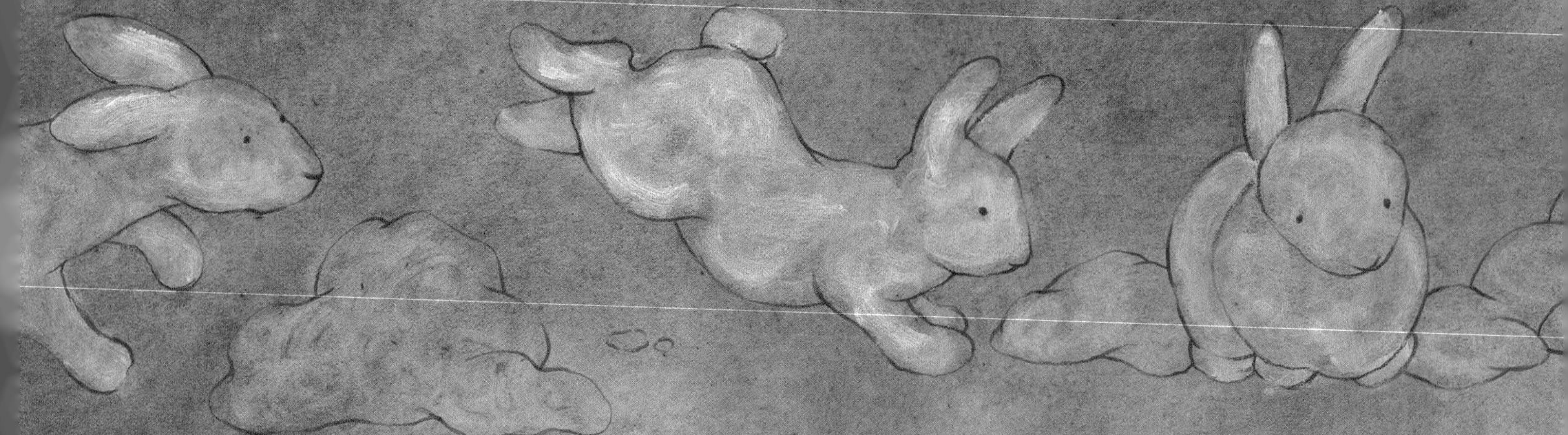

Then Rag Baby saw them. Next to the wall. Gray and round and shadowy. Hunched in bunches. "Dust Bunnies!" whispered Rag Baby.

The Dust Bunnies did not move as Rag Baby came closer.

"They're sleeping," he said. They were so still and peaceful, and Rag Baby was so sleepy himself, that he curled up beside them and fell asleep.

A sweeping sound woke Rag Baby the next morning. He jumped up and saw that he had been sleeping beside fuzzy balls of dust. "So that's a Dust Bunny!" he said. "Wait until Cat-Cat and Bella Elephant hear this!"

But just then a bunch of broom bristles swept down on him. Gray, musty dust covered him. A piece of paper flew over him. Then the Dust Bunnies, the paper, and Rag Baby were swept into a dustpan and dumped into a trash bag. More papers, a shoe box, some gum wrappers, and an old sock came tumbling in on top of them.

Rag Baby scrambled to the top of the trash and jumped up with all his might. Out of the bag he came. But instead of landing on the floor, he landed in a box of clothes. Before he could climb out, the lid was slapped down on top of the box, and Rag Baby was trapped!

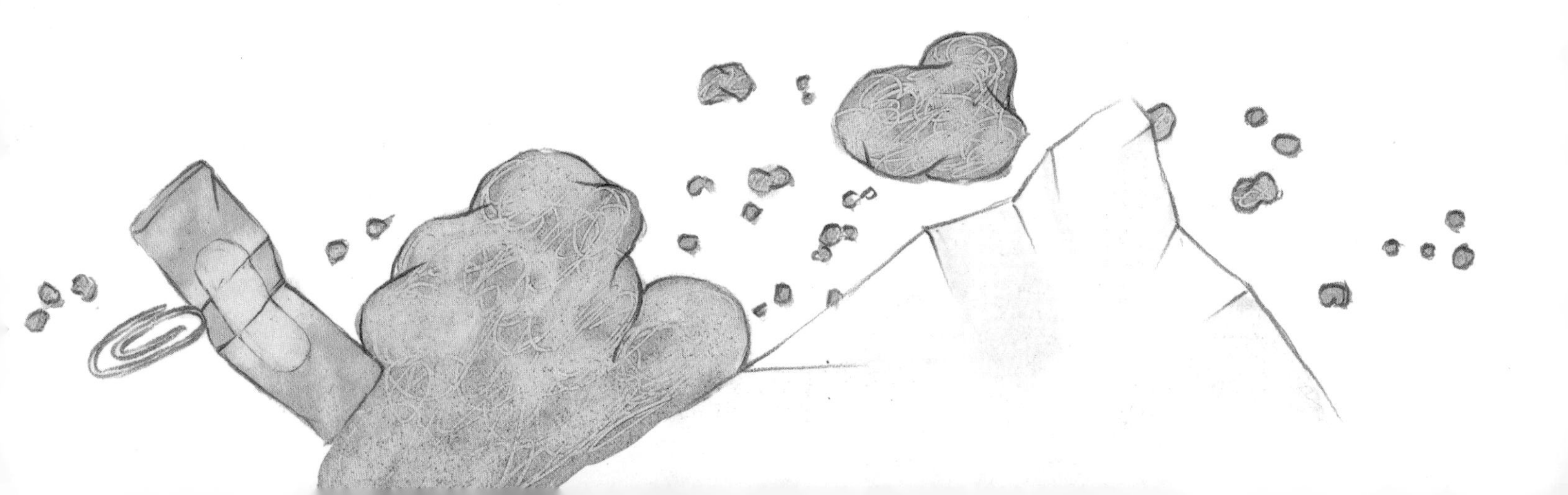

Through a small hole in the box, Rag Baby saw that he was being carried to the car. The car took the box to a big truck. *Look at me!* thought Rag Baby. *I'm going to go on an adventure of my own!* Then he had a second thought. *What will Jessie say when she sees that I'm gone? Oh, I wish Jessie was here right now! I'm not sure I like this adventure.*

The truck chugged and bumped down the street. It took the box across town.

Rag Baby found himself in a building with a lot of old clothes. He soon learned that it was a store where used clothes were sold. There a man took the lid off the box and began pulling out the clothes Jessie had outgrown.

Then the man pulled out Rag Baby. "What's this?" he asked. "Looks like a rag doll," said a lady. "Put it with the toys."

So the man tied a price tag around Rag Baby's arm. Then he placed Rag Baby on a shelf with the other toys in the store.

There Rag Baby sat. And sat. And sat. Day after day. Rag Baby passed the time watching the people who came into the store. The bell on the door jingled as they came in. They all looked at the clothes, and most of them looked at the toys. They bought toys from the shelf *below* Rag Baby. They bought toys from the shelf *above* Rag Baby. They even bought toys that sat *beside* Rag Baby. But they didn't buy Rag Baby.

Rag Baby was sad. He missed Bella Elephant and Cat-Cat and, most of all, Jessie.

Summer changed into autumn. Autumn changed into winter. Then one snowy day the bell on the shop door jingled. Rag Baby looked up. What he saw made him want to jump off the shelf. It was Jessie! She had her backpack, and she wore her favorite red-and-yellow-striped winter scarf. *Look over here, Jessie!* Rag Baby thought. *Please look over here!*

But at that very moment, the man who worked at the store came to wash the counter. He set a bucket of sudsy water on the floor. Then he scowled and mumbled, "Forgot my washrag!" He looked around and grabbed Rag Baby. "Might as well use this," he said. "Nobody will ever buy it anyway."

The man dipped Rag Baby into the sudsy water, lifted him out dripping wet, and started to squeeze him out over the bucket.

It was then that Jessie saw Rag Baby!

"Wait!" Jessie called. She ran up to the man. "Wait! I want to buy that rag doll. That's my very own Rag Baby!"

She added softly, "I thought he was lost forever. I just have to get him back."

The man scowled. "This thing is important to you?" he asked.

"Yes," said Jessie. "I want to buy him."

The man held up the soggy price tag. "Here's the price," he said.

Jessie frowned. She dug through all the pockets in her backpack. Then she held out a handful of coins. "Here's all I have. Can I have him for this much?" she asked.

"Sorry," said the man. "That's not enough." He squeezed Rag Baby's tummy, and Rag Baby could tell he was about to be wrung out.

Jessie bit her lip. "Wait!" she said. She wrapped her fingers around the end of her soft, warm scarf.

Rag Baby took a deep breath. He knew how much that scarf meant to Jessie. It was the only one she'd ever worn. It was special because it had been made by Grandma.

Jessie pulled the scarf off and held it out to the man. "How about the money and this?"

The man plopped Rag Baby on the counter, wiped his hands on his jeans, and took the scarf. "All right," he said. "This will be easier to sell than an old rag doll."

Jessie put her money on the counter and picked up Rag Baby. She gently squeezed the water out of his soggy, pudgy tummy and took him right home.

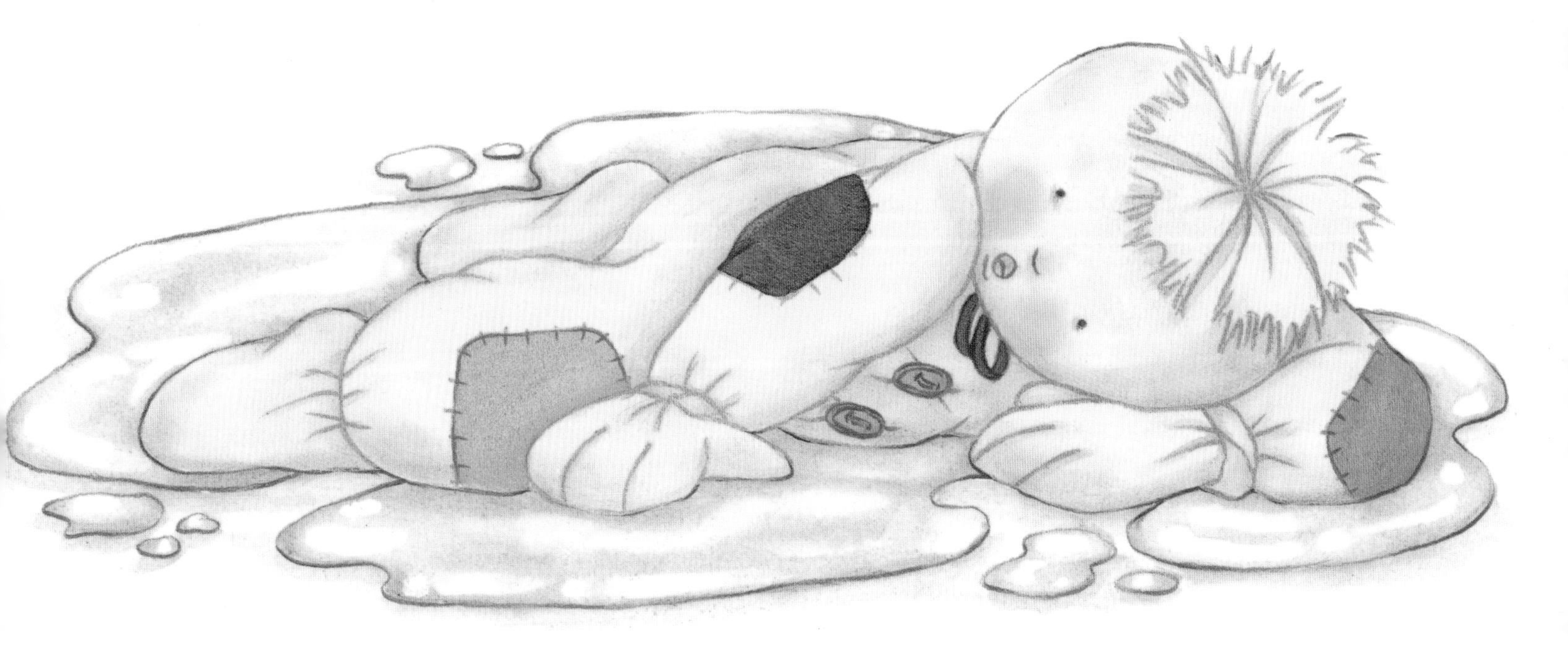

Rag Baby was so happy to be with Jessie again that he didn't care that he was wet. Neither did Jessie. She hugged him close all the way home.

Jessie set Rag Baby beside her as she read a book in front of the warm fire. When Rag Baby was dry, Jessie kissed him and placed him back on her bed between Cat-Cat and Bella Elephant.

"Welcome home," whispered Bella Elephant.

"We thought we'd never see you again," said Cat-Cat.

Rag Baby told them all about his adventure. Little by little, every toy in Jessie's room heard how Jessie gave up the scarf Grandma had made. They heard that she gave it up to save Rag Baby—to buy him back.

When Jessie grew up, she gave Rag Baby as a very special present to her children. She often told them about giving her one and only winter scarf to buy her Rag Baby back. Then she would say, "Remember: God loved you so much that he gave Jesus, his only Son, to buy you for himself. He did it because you were made to belong to him. And he will never stop loving you because he wants you to be part of his family forever and ever."